D0537001

Red Cloud's War

Brave Eagle's Account of
the Fetterman Fight

December 21, 1866

Bozeman

Virginia City

M O N T A N A

Fort C.F. Smith

Fort Phil Kearny

W Y O M I N G

Fort Reno

Bozeman Trail

Oregon Trail

Fort Laramie

to VIRGINIA CITY

Peno Head

Peno Creek

FETTERMAN FIGHT

North Piney Creek

Lodge Trail

Ambush Hill

BIGHORN

lumber camp

Piney Island

South Piney Creek

Wagon-Box Fight
2 Aug 1867

Sullivant Hills

Ridge

MOUNTAINS

Decoys

wood train attacked

Fetterman

N

Little Piney Creek

wood road

dry creek

dry creek

one mile

Red Cloud's War

Brave Eagle's Account of the Fetterman Fight
December 21, 1866

Told & Illustrated by
Paul Goble

Foreword by
Robert Lewis

Wisdom Tales

Prairie Dog Creek

BOZEMAN TRAIL

badlands

FORT PHIL KEARNY
cemetery
Pilot Hill   lookout

Big Piney Creek

to FORT LARAMIE

For Edgar Red Cloud,
great-grandson of the Chief.

Ate ciyuonihan kin,
cajemayakage cin on wopila eciciye wacin;
canke wowapi cikala kin le cicu.
Wakinyan Cikala he miye.

Author's Note

What is known of the fight was told in later years by the Indians who had fought in it, and so it seems appropriate that it should be retold by them. Although Brave Eagle's account is fiction, it attempts to capture the spirit of the published Indian accounts, but because Indians told only what they saw and did, it has also been necessary to draw on the material of white historians, in order to give the reader a better understanding of the fight and the events which preceded it. Many of the words spoken by Red Cloud in this account are edited extracts from his recorded speeches.

When the opportunity presented itself to produce this special edition of the book, I jumped at the chance. Its shorter page count and modified layout are closer to my original ideas for the book, and for the first time the illustrations are in glorious digitized color. The original artwork has recently been added to the collections in the South Dakota Art Museum, after being stored for the last forty years in my brother's attic in England. I'm grateful to him, and to Lisa Scholten and Gregory Bryan for all of their assistance in this matter.

Red Cloud's War: Brave Eagle's Account of the Fetterman Fight
© Paul Goble, 2015
Wisdom Tales is an imprint of World Wisdom, Inc.
Wisdom Tales wishes to thank the South Dakota Art Museum for their assistance in the loan and scanning of the original artwork of this title.

Printed in China on acid-free paper.
Production Date: February 2015, Plant & Location: Printed by 1010 Printing International Ltd, Job/Batch # TT15010457
Library of Congress Cataloging-in-Publication Data
Goble, Paul.
  [Brave Eagle's account of the Fetterman Fight.]
  Red Cloud's War : Brave Eagle's account of the Fetterman Fight / told & illustrated by Paul Goble ; foreword by Robert Lewis. -- Revised and updated edition.
      pages cm
  Previous edition: The Hundred in the Hands: Brave Eagle's Account of the Fetterman Fight, 21st December 1866 / Paul and Dorothy Goble. New York : Bradbury Press, 1972.
  Includes bibliographical references.
  Audience: Grades 4-6.
  ISBN 978-1-937786-38-0 (casebound : alk. paper) 1. Fetterman Fight, Wyo., 1866--Juvenile literature. 2. Oglala Indians--Wars--Juvenile literature. 3. Red Cloud, 1822-1909--Juvenile literature. I. Goble, Paul, illustrator. II. Title. III. Title: Brave Eagle's account of the Fetterman Fight.
  E83.866.G62 2015
  978.0049752440092--dc23
                                                                                                                2014048349

For information address Wisdom Tales, P.O. Box 2682, Bloomington, Indiana 47402-2682
www.wisdomtalespress.com

Foreword

Being a native storyteller, I have had the unique and privileged opportunity of bringing my people's legends into being by voicing those stories whose meaning resides within each of us.

In reading Paul Goble's *Red Cloud's War*, I am reminded again of the power of stories. These moments that have passed—whether pleasant with beauty or boiling with injustice done and never rectified—they become stories, become history. They remain inside of us like dreams that need to be remembered. Paul Goble has found one of those dreams and with poignant words given a new vision of Red Cloud's War, looking through the eyes of Brave Eagle.

I hope you will find echoes of Brave Eagle inside yourself as he travels over a changing world with courage. I ask you to follow with me and hear once again the drumbeats and songs of the plains with the beautiful art and words of *Red Cloud's War*. Follow those hoof beats and heartbeats, creating pathways into your soul. Come follow that pathway into Brave Eagle's being with Paul Goble's very own words echoing inside your own heart and breathing life into history.

Robert Lewis
Cherokee, Navaho, and Apache storyteller

"*The white men have surrounded me and have left me nothing but an island. When we first had this land we were strong, now our nation is melting away like snow on the hill-sides where the sun is warm; while the white people grow like blades of grass when summer is coming. I do not want the white people to make any roads through our country.*"

Red Cloud

The Background

In 1866 the process of driving the Indians from their lands was nearing its final stages. The Civil War had ended and the nation's resources were directed toward healing the wounds inflicted during the five terrible years. While reconstruction was going on, the authorities in Washington hoped they could avoid military conflict with the Indian tribes, but at the same time they realized nothing could halt the civilian expansion westward.

The powerful Sioux and Cheyenne posed the greatest threat; the administration decided it would be cheaper to appease them, if possible, than to fight them. A commission was sent out to Fort Laramie in June to make peace and to give presents to the Indians; at the same time the commission hoped to secure the Indians' agreement to a right of way through their lands. The right of way which they wanted was the Bozeman Trail leading to the gold mines of Virginia City farther to the west. It was the shortest route and had been unofficially used for several years, but at great risk of Indian attacks.

Red Cloud, war chief of the Oglala Sioux, and many other chiefs, were determined to prohibit the use of the trail.

Whether the commission would succeed or fail in its attempt to gain the Indians' assent, Washington had already decided to give military protection to civilians who wished to use the trail. Colonel Henry Carrington, with seven hundred men, was ordered to build forts along the trail, to protect it.

Having obtained the agreement of a few peaceful chiefs, they returned to Washington and declared the Bozeman Trail open and safe for travel. They had grossly underestimated the Indians' determination. At no time, even after the forts had been built, was travel safe, and for long periods the trail was quite impassable. Far from giving protection, the soldiers could do no more than protect themselves inside their own forts. Within six months after the commission left Fort Laramie, the army suffered its worst defeat by the Indians, up to that time, in an engagement known as the Fetterman Fight.

Brave Eagle Begins

I was just nineteen years old that spring when Big Ribs and some of our people who were living around Fort Laramie came to our camp on Powder River. They said that white men had come from the Great White Father in Washington and they wanted to smoke the pipe with our chiefs and make peace. "They are important men," Big Ribs said, "dressed in black suits and tall shiny hats. Those who want to be friends, these white men say, should come at once and make their mark on a piece of paper. They will give a great feast for all the people and more presents than you can carry home with you." *Ho!* "Guns and plenty of ammunition as well." *Washtay!* Good!

"Tell the white men," Red Cloud answered Big Ribs, "that the bands of my people are scattered far and that our horses are too weak after the long winter to travel now. But tell them that we shall be at the Soldiers' Town before two moons have passed and that we will come in peace with our women and little children."

There was talking and arguing in the camps for many days about whether we should go to Fort Laramie. Sitting Bull and Crazy Horse said they would not go and there were many among us who agreed. Crazy Horse said, "The white men will tell you that the land they have is not enough and that you must give them more, and they will make you touch the pen. Do not trust the white men; they are never satisfied with what they have. Remember that the Great Spirit gave this land to the Oglalas and one does not sell the earth upon which the people walk."

The chiefs and warriors talked. I hoped we would go because I wanted some of the white man's food which our relatives, the stay-around-the-fort people, spoke so much about.

And we went as Red Cloud had said we would. We traveled slowly, with the bands spread out because there were no enemies to be feared, and we camped where there was good grass for the horses at night. When we were near Fort Laramie the soldiers came out to meet us, marching in long lines with those in front making music. They led us to where the stay-around-the-fort people were camped, and the women set up the tipis next to them.

Everyone was happy. At last peace would be made with the white man. There had been war between us for as long as I could remember.

The women were excited to see great piles of presents being unloaded for us from wagons onto a flat place beyond the camp. The soldiers who were guarding them said there were many fine things for the women, and guns for us as well. It was difficult to wait.

The council started the next day.

The white men talked among themselves as white people always do, talking all together and not really listening to what the others say.

When the pipe had been lit, Red Cloud rose. He raised it in silent prayer to the sky above and touched it to the earth beneath. The pipe was then passed around the circle and when all had smoked, Red Cloud spoke what was in all our hearts:

"My brothers and my friends, the Great Spirit placed me and my people on this land. When the white men first came we gave them some of our land and we did not wish to hurt them. But the white people wanted more and drove us back and took more land. Now you have come from the Great White Father and have offered us peace, and we are happy. If I had not wanted peace as well, I should not have come here. But the Great White Father must tell his children to keep the peace; if they had not come into our lands there never would have been any trouble between us. You have your land fenced in and you do not want us to come on it. We, too, do not want you to bother us. I want peace. I speak for all my people."

They came, marching with guns and long knives, and holding high their flags. They came with saws and axes to cut down the trees, and spades to dig up the earth; they came with white-topped wagons with wheels which squeaked, and with the great wagon guns which speak twice. They came with horse soldiers and walking-soldiers, singing as they marched, saying in their songs that they would drive us like buffalo before them and kill us all. With them rode a young soldier-chief, Captain Brown, who laughed much, saying that he would bring back Red Cloud's scalp. And with him rode another chief, Captain Fetterman, who boasted loudly for all to hear that he could whip the whole Sioux Nation with only eighty men. It was brave talk, yet foolish.

We went back to the council the next day and Red Cloud spoke for the last time:

"It must be either peace or war. If you want peace, return at once." Pointing at Colonel Carrington, he said, "The Great White Father sends us presents and wants us to sell him the trail, but you come with soldiers to steal it before we say yes or no! You must understand that the Sioux, and especially the Oglalas, have many warriors.

"We are brave and ready to fight for our lands. We are not afraid of your men, nor of the young soldier-chief who threatens and makes big boast of killing us all with only eighty men. Many warriors are ready to meet you. Every family will send its young men and they all will say of the Great White Father's dogs, 'Let them come!'

"I will talk with you no more. I will go now and I will fight you. As long as I live, I will fight you for the last hunting grounds of my people."

We left Fort Laramie after that because we knew there was going to be trouble. Sitting Bull and Crazy Horse had been right; we should never have gone to talk with the white men. I was young then and I did not understand all these things. I remember I was thinking most about the presents and the guns we never had and the white man's food I did not eat. But when I look back now, I know Red Cloud was right not to take the presents; he would not sell our lands for a few pretty things to give to his wife. He was a great chief who always decided what was best for his people.

Red Cloud led us north to the mouth of Prairie Dog Creek. It was the Moon of Ripening Cherries, July, the time when we hold our Sun Dance every year. It is then that the sun begins to go back from its highest place in the sky and the time of year when the sage covering the prairie is fully grown and the buffalo roll their great bodies in its fragrant leaves. In the Sun Dance we join the whole universe in rejoicing and giving thanks.

I think we had all forgotten about the soldiers during those happy days. Yet it was not long afterwards that scouts came into camp bringing news that the soldiers were already building a fort (Fort Phil Kearny) on the Piney Fork of Powder River, about an easy day's ride south of our camp. When Red Cloud heard this he sent out runners to the Miniconjous and to our allies the Cheyennes and Arapahoes, calling them to a council of war.

It was one of the greatest gatherings of the tribes in the memory of the old men. I was not a chief in those days and I did not go to sit outside the council tipi. I heard later that every chief had spoken for war against the soldiers and that they had all smoked the war pipe.

There were many small fights that summer, but no great victory.

One early morning, before the soldiers were really awake, we drove off all their horses. We drove them hard and they were tired by the time we drove them around the camp circle.

All the people came running from the tipis to see, the women making the tremolo and the young boys shouting and laughing as they jumped on the soldiers' horses and galloped them round and round the camp. The warriors and the old men came forward to look and to examine the iron shoes and to wonder over the marks burnt with hot irons into the horses' flanks. Everyone was happy, and we felt proud when Red Cloud told us it was a good thing we had done.

All through the summer we made life hard for them. If the soldiers wanted water from the creek, they had to fight for it. If they wanted timber for their houses from the forests, or grass for their horses from the valley bottom, they gave their blood for it. If they needed food from Fort Laramie, they had to fight their way up the trail. And if they hunted fresh meat, their hunters returned more hunted than hunting. We made them prisoners inside their own fort.

Late in the Moon of Falling Leaves, November, when the buffalo hunts were over and the meat packs were filled for the winter, the hunting bands of the Oglalas and the Miniconjous came together again. We tried to draw the soldiers away from the shadow of their fort with the great guns which looked out through holes in the fence. We could not fight against those with bows and arrows, tomahawks and knives. Red Cloud sent out warriors as decoys to draw the soldiers away to a place among the hills where more warriors waited, hiding in ambush. But the soldiers would not follow. The days passed, and our young men became impatient with waiting so long.

Then one day the soldiers did follow the decoys led by Crazy Horse. It was the young soldier-chief, Captain Fetterman, who led the soldiers and they followed the decoys almost into our ambush, when some of our young impatient ones started shooting too soon. We chased them back into the fort, but the plan to trap them had failed and the chiefs were angry with the young men.

The winter was moving south and soon it would be too cold to fight the soldiers again that year. The mornings were bright and clear and the Big Horn Mountains, with new snow in the high meadows, seemed only a short ride away to the west. Already the trees stood bare beside creeks and the birds searched hurriedly for little things to eat among the dead leaves soon to be frozen over.

Red Cloud talked with the chiefs. He planned to try once again to draw the soldiers into the hills. But many shook their heads. "Now the soldiers know our plan and they will not follow the decoys a second time." I, too, did not think the young soldier-chief would be so foolish as to walk again into the trap. "Then let us ask the medicine-man who has far-seeing eyes to see what is to be," said Red Cloud. "Let him tell us."

And so the medicine-man was called to the council tipi. I had been frightened of this mysterious person when a boy, because he always dressed in women's clothes, but he was much respected by the tribes for his great powers of making magic and looking into the future. Word spread quickly around the camp that he had ridden out into the hills, looking with inward eyes to foretell whether we would kill any soldiers. People gathered to hear what he would say.

After a little while he rode back to where the chiefs were waiting, sitting on their horses. "I have ten dead soldiers, five in each hand," he said, stretching his arms before him, "Do you want them?" Red Cloud was angry. "Do you not see," he said, "that there are many too many warriors here to share so few soldiers?" and he whipped the medicine-man's horse away, telling him to look for a great victory with many dead soldiers. Three times the medicine-man returned, and each time Red Cloud sent him away to look again. He was gone a long time and I wondered what he would foretell.

Perhaps he was frightened of Red Cloud and did not say what he really saw. And then he came, a fourth time, galloping down from a hill behind us, blowing shrill notes on an eagle-bone whistle. He fell from his horse in front of the chiefs and said, "I have a hundred dead soldiers in my hands," and at that everyone cheered. It was what we had been waiting for, and everyone ran forward, trying to be the first to touch the enemy held in the hollow of his hands. The medicine-man had said it, and he was never wrong. And the fight we were to have with the soldiers the next day is still remembered as the Battle of the Hundred in the Hands.

We left camp early. It was cold, with a wind which had a feeling of snow coming, and the sun shone without warmth between dark cloud ridges. There was ice on the creek, and the sparkling grass and dead leaves crackled under our horses' hooves. White men have often asked how many there were that day fighting the soldiers. I do not know. There were very many. Maybe a man could have gone on counting until he reached almost one thousand.

We stopped where the white man's trail comes down the steep ridge of Ambush Hill into the narrow valley of Peno Creek. It was there that the soldiers had nearly been trapped a few days before. Red Cloud sent warriors ahead to attack the wagons used for hauling timber. When the warriors saw the soldiers coming out of the fort to defend the wagons, they were to retreat and leave the decoys to coax the soldiers into our ambush. It was a difficult and dangerous thing the decoys had to do.

The chiefs rode along the hills telling the young men to stay hidden and not to shoot until the signal was given. This time there must be no mistake. Little Horse, the Cheyenne chief who had made a vow not to retreat in the fight, would give the signal. When he stood up and waved his lance above his head, then would be the moment.

I looked up at the sky and the rolling clouds and I knew snow was coming. We sat still as the rocks around us.

A shot! Then more, far off! It was the warriors attacking the wagons. After a while there was silence, and more waiting. Perhaps the soldiers would not follow the decoys after all. An eagle shrieked as he glided with curling wingtips low along the ridge. It was a sign; had he seen the soldiers coming? He flies higher than all other birds and sees everything that moves below him.

When it was seen from the fort that the wood train was under attack, Captain Fetterman was ordered to go and relieve it. His contempt for the Indians' fighting ability was well known and Colonel Carrington had misgivings about sending him. His orders were explicit: "Support the wood train. Relieve it and report to me. Do not engage or pursue Indians at its expense. Under no circumstances pursue over Lodge Trail Ridge." The orders were read out and then repeated before they were handed over in writing.

Instead of advancing directly along the wood road to relieve the wagon train, Captain Fetterman led his force behind Sullivant Hills, with the evident intention of crossing over the hills and attacking the Indians from the rear. When the Indian scouts on Sullivant Hills saw Fetterman's advance, they signaled the warriors attacking the wood train to withdraw. They separated, the main party retreating north, leaving the decoys to entice the soldiers into the ambush. Captain Fetterman had orders not to pursue the Indians, but he now had eighty-two men under his command, sufficient for him to gain the glory he was seeking.

After what seemed a long time there were more shots, always a little closer as the decoys drew the soldiers toward us. I slipped my bow from its case and strung it ready. My horse was restless; he, too, knew there was going to be a fight. I took his head between my hands and spoke to him softly, "We are in danger; obey me in everything. If you have to run for your life and mine, do your best, and if we return I shall give you an eagle feather to tie in your mane." He was quiet after that. All the warriors were making ready, pulling the covers from their shields and tying their buffalo robes around their waists. My cousin, Slow Buffalo, stood next to me, whistling his medicine song through his teeth to strengthen his heart.

There they are! Ten warriors standing against the sky and shooting back at soldiers close behind them. See, it is the young soldier-chief, Captain Fetterman, who holds up his arm for them to stop up there on the ridge. This time he leads eighty soldiers, and more.

The decoys charged up close under the soldiers' guns. Crazy Horse was leading. Another, a Cheyenne, seemed to ride right among the soldiers until I thought he would be hit. A soldier toppled from his saddle, and then the decoys were galloping back again, down toward the trail to make the soldiers follow.

The soldiers advanced, their horses picking their way carefully down the steep slope, with the walking soldiers marching in lines behind. We held our horses' mouths so they would not neigh at the strange horses. Will the young ones hold back a little longer? Everything is still; there is only the creak of saddles and the clink of iron horseshoes against the stones and hard frozen earth. The leading soldiers have reached the trail. Now they are between us. Little Horse, who will give the signal, still has not moved. I pull the arrow tighter against the bowstring. The decoys have turned around and are climbing back again, up the trail toward the soldiers. It is time!

There! Little Horse shakes his lance above his head. I jerk the arrow back and it flies from my bow and then is lost among the hundreds joining it. My second arrow follows quickly before the first has hit, and after it another, and then another joins the cloud of arrows falling like wind-whipped hailstones among and all around the soldiers down there on the trail. The sound of all those arrows comes back even now to my ears; it is a sound like no other sound I have ever heard and it is bad to remember. It is mixed up with many guns going off and people shouting, the sound of horses and men in agony, and above it all the sharp notes of the bugle many times repeated.

I think the soldiers were too surprised and frightened to shoot back. For a long moment they stood, not knowing what to do. They did not have a chance. Many died right there before they had fired their first shot. If our arrows missed one soldier, then the other next to him would fall because they were bunched up together in lines where they had stopped. I remember seeing a horse with arrows sticking in him and crazy with pain break from the lines and charge off down the trail straight into the decoys. The soldier tried desperately to rein him back, but fell from the saddle full of arrows; his horse dragged him bumping over the frozen earth. It was bad.

And then all the soldiers turned and were running, running back up the trail toward the fort, the horse-soldiers leaving the walking-soldiers behind. Everything happened fast. I joined the warriors rushing down on both sides toward the blue lines of soldiers on the trail. Suddenly those near me were shouting to stop and everyone was jerking back on the reins and bumping into those in front; arrows, shot by our friends on the other side of the trail, were whistling among us. Ghost Wolf, out in front, had fallen with an arrow sticking through his neck. We rode back quickly, out of the way, and skirted behind the soldiers.

The horse-soldiers left the trail and climbed up the side where the Cheyennes had been hiding. They kept close together; our arrows could not miss them. Soldiers always fight that way; they do not zig-zag their horses to avoid being hit. It is a strange way to fight and stay alive. But they fought bravely. Many fell on the way and those who reached the jutting rocks of the ridge were surrounded by the Cheyennes. It was the same with the walking-soldiers. They scrambled after the horse-soldiers, turning and dropping onto one knee to shoot back. They fought hard all the way; the dead and wounded littered their tracks up the ravine. They never did catch up with the horse-soldiers; they turned to fight where there are some large rocks standing in a circle.

I remember well how one brave soldier, with long hair on his face, gave his life so that the others could have time to climb higher up the ridge. The story has been told many times. He had a many-shot pistol in each hand and was pointing them first at one of us, and then at another, and jumping from side to side and shouting with the biggest voice I have ever heard. He fought more like an Indian than a white man and it seemed that our arrows could not touch him. It was that solider who killed Fearless Bear and Red Eagle. When he had no more bullets left, Charging Eagle, an Oglala chief, rode up and shot an arrow into him. But the solider did not fall. He was hard to kill. He broke off the arrow where it was sticking in his shoulder and, running forward, he pulled Charging Eagle out of his saddle and killed him.

The sky was like night coming, with snow driving hard across the valley. The walking-soldiers were well hidden among the gray rocks. Above where they were hiding, their flag flapped like something alive in the wind, a bit of bright color against the dark earth. I could just see their white faces as they took aim over the rocks, and the puffs of gun smoke and frozen breath whipped away up the valley with the slanting snow.

Red Cloud was in the front shouting, "Let's get it done; only the rocks live forever," and we charged right up to the circle of rocks, shooting in among the soldiers. But their guns were too many for us and we had to go back. Several riders were already down.

After that every warrior left his horse to crawl up to the soldiers and surround them. I was so cold that I could not feel my fingers against the bowstring. Then High Backbone, war-chief of the Miniconjous, got up and started running, shouting for us to follow. "Now is a good time to die!" *Hoka Hey!* We were all running up among the rocks and jumping from side to side to dodge soldiers' bullets. I was just behind the leading ones and for a moment I could not see the soldiers, but then the few who were left alive were up and we were fighting them hand to hand. High Backbone was first among them. He struck like lightning to left and right around him and I saw a soldier fall beneath his heavy stone-headed tomahawk.

A soldier rose up right in front of me. I did not have time to shoot. He raised his empty gun above his head and I jumped aside as it shattered on the rocks where I had been. He shouted something in white-man talk which I did not understand. He was picking up a stone to throw at me when I knocked him forward with my bow.

There were only a few more shots up under the ridge where the Cheyennes were fighting the last of the horse-soldiers. My arrows were all gone and I did not join them. Then suddenly there was shouting, and a soldier who was not dead was up again and fighting with Swift Hawk. The soldier had lost his gun and had only a bugle for a club. I do not think Swift Hawk felt brave when he stabbed him with his knife. We saw that he was an old man who should have stayed back beside his fire while his grandchildren fought. He had died bravely, and a warrior covered his body with a buffalo robe.

It was all over. But a dog nobody had noticed before and which had come with the soldiers ran whimpering up the trail toward the fort. He ran, looking back for those who would never follow him again. "Let him tell the other dogs at the fort what has happened here," said Red Cloud. But nothing was to return that day, and he fell with an arrow through his body, a small and silent thing among the rocks and snow.

Everyone picked up the guns which were lying around. I found one, and we searched for ammunition among the dead soldiers. I pulled off a soldier's blue coat with brass buttons. Inside the pocket there was a knife which folded up. It was pretty, with a handle made of shell and a long chain hanging from one end.

We looked at the dead soldiers and at their two young chiefs lying close together. They looked very young to lead so many men; we too have had young chiefs who were foolish in their bravery.

It was a great victory. It had been just as the medicine-man had foretold.

Brave Eagle Ends

Standing on that peaceful and beautiful hill today there is a monument which the white people have built to remember their dead soldiers. Men and women and little children climb from the road to read the writing on the metal shield and to be photographed beside the monument. They stand, smiling and unthinking on the earth and the growing grass which remembers the warm blood of those brave soldiers spilled there that day.

I have sent my heart back over the years; the fight has come back as from the dead, but now it has been retold, it will go back to the dead to remain forever.

There is no more to say.

"*Red Cloud's War is the only instance in the history of the United States where the government has gone to war and afterwards negotiated a peace conceding everything demanded by the enemy and exacting nothing in return.*"

Doane Robinson
(*State Historian of South Dakota*)

Conclusion

Throughout the summer of 1867 the siege continued, and no white men dared to use the Bozeman Trail. A similar state of siege existed at the other forts along the trail. The army, trained to fight conventional pitched battles, had not learned to fight an enemy who employs hit-and-run tactics. The soldiers left the forts only when it was necessary to cut grass or timber. It was on such an occasion, on August 2, 1867, that Captain Powell and twenty-eight soldiers guarding the woodcutters, were attacked by an overwhelming force of Red Cloud's warriors. The soldiers had just been issued with new breech-loading rifles, and it was these "medicine guns," as the Indians called them, which enabled the soldiers to defend themselves successfully. The Wagon Box Fight was a defeat for the Indians, but it confirmed Washington's fears that Red Cloud was determined to continue the siege.

The army was still smarting from its defeat in the Fetterman Fight and further humiliated by the inability of its forces to defend the Bozeman Trail. The generals were eager to launch a massive campaign against the Sioux, but Washington realized that such an offensive would be costly and long-drawn-out and they were not prepared to sanction it. Instead, they ordered the forts to be abandoned. By the Treaty of 1868 the Bozeman Trail was closed and the Powder River country given back to the Indians. It was a triumph for Red Cloud.

The land for which he had fought so hard was solemnly promised to his people forever. He had succeeded in holding back the white people for a time, but he knew his people could never win the final struggle soon to come.

Washington soon forgot the treaty and the soldiers marched again, but Red Cloud never went back on the promise he had given to fight no more.

References

Television, films, and popular novels have given a mainly wrong impression of the Plains Indians, and because the more reliable books may not be so well known to the general reader, this list is included.

Accounts of the Fetterman Fight can be found in the following books:

Andrist, Ralph K. *The Long Death: The Last Days of the Plains Indians*. Norman: University of Oklahoma Press, 2001.

Grinnell, George B. *The Fighting Cheyennes*. Norman: University of Oklahoma Press, 1983.

Hyde, George E. *Red Cloud's Folk: A History of the Oglala Sioux Indians*. Norman: University of Oklahoma Press, 1979.

Neihardt, John G. *Black Elk Speaks: Being the Life Story of a Holy Man of the Oglala Sioux*. Lincoln: University of Nebraska Press, 1988.

————. *When the Tree Flowered: The Fictional Autobiography of Eagle Voice, a Sioux Indian*. Lincoln: University of Nebraska Press, 1991.

Olson, James C. *Red Cloud and the Sioux Problem*. Lincoln: University of Nebraska Press, 1965.

Robinson, Doane. *History of the Dakota or Sioux Indians*. Minneapolis: Ross & Haines, 1956.

Sandoz, Mari. *Crazy Horse: The Strange Man of the Oglalas*. Lincoln: University of Nebraska Press, 1992.

Schmitt, Martin F. & Brown, Dee. *Fighting Indians of the West*. New York: Charles Scribner's, 1948.

Stands in Timber, John & Liberty, Margot. *Cheyenne Memories*. New Haven: Yale University, 1998.

For a better understanding of the ways of the Plains Indians and the Sioux and Cheyenne tribes in particular, the following books are recommended:

Blish, Helen H. *A Pictographic History of the Oglala Sioux: The Drawings of Amos Bad Heart Bull*. Lincoln: University of Nebraska Press, 1967.

Brown, Joseph E. *The Sacred Pipe: Black Elk's Account of the Seven Rites of the Oglala Sioux*. Norman: University of Oklahoma Press, 1989.

Cohoe, William. *A Cheyenne Sketchbook*. Norman: University of Oklahoma Press, 1964.

Densmore, Frances. *Teton Sioux Music*. Lincoln: University of Nebraska Press, 1992.

Eastman, Charles (Ohiyesa). *Living in Two Worlds: The American Indian Experience*. Bloomington: World Wisdom, 2010.

Fitzgerald, Michael (ed.). *The Essential Charles Eastman (Ohiyesa): Light on the Indian World*. Bloomington: World Wisdom, 2007.

Grinnell, George B. *The Cheyenne Indians: Their History and Lifeways*. New York: Cooper Square Publishers, Inc., 1964; Bloomington: World Wisdom, 2008.

Laubin, Reginald & Gladys. *The Indian Tipi: Its History, Construction, and Use*. Norman: University of Oklahoma Press, 1989.

Lyford, Carrie A. *Quill and Beadwork of the Western Sioux*. Bureau of Indian Affairs, 1954.

Marquis, Thomas B. *Wooden Leg: A Warrior Who Fought Custer*. Lincoln: University of Nebraska Press, 2003.

Standing Bear, Luther. *My People, the Sioux*. Lincoln: University of Nebraska Press, 2006.

————. *My Indian Boyhood*. Lincoln: University of Nebraska Press, 2006.